PRAIS

"I don't think that there is now, in Mexico, a literary mind more original than Daniela Tarazona's. Her books are as disconcerting as they are brilliant. Her ability to generate powerful, enigmatic images in the brains of her readers, dazzling."

—Álvaro Enrigue, author of *Sudden Death*

"This is a novel about the electricity that inhabits us, sometimes predictably, sometimes like a lightning storm in the brain. It is also about a writer's relationship with her mother and about how fragile memory and language are. But above all it is about the terrible lucidity that comes with being abnormal, and how poetry is the only science that allows us to understand what someone with that lucidity sees."

—Yuri Herrera, author of *Ten Planets*

"The metamorphosis undertaken by Daniela Tarazona in *Divided Island* reaches its full form here, which, paradoxically, is not a form but rather its dissolution: a way of disappearing in words. The author has become writing. In her place, another woman who is pure language has left for an island with the intention of committing suicide. Or rather, a woman—the same, another, which one, none—has not left for an island . . . I happen to understand and not understand this book. But it is in what I do not understand where I can best experience its atrocious lucidity as a chill of beauty and truth."

—Luis Felipe Fabre, author of *Recital of the Dark Verses*

"Closer to Lispector, Elizondo, and Robbe-Grillet, as well as poetry as a concretion and reflection of the dissolution of the world, *Divided Island* traps us in its mystery without letting us go."
—Ana García Bergua, *Letras Libres*

"Daniela Tarazona's aesthetic appeals to the profound, to the power of evocation in literature. Magnificent, difficult, full of emotion and meaning."
—Sara Poot Herrera, Andrea Jeftanovic, and Daniel Centeno Maldonado, Jury of the Sor Juana Inés de la Cruz Prize 2022

"It is the complexity of the writing of this book, its poetic dimension, that immerses us in the anxiety of living to such a degree that we want to die." —Adriana Pacheco, *Hablemos Escritoras*

"This is writing to the limit, which is drawn on the sand of that island where Tarazona takes us and where we must allow ourselves to be led without logic or linearity, as when we are before a poem: surrendering ourselves to its mystery." —Alfredo Núñez Lanz, *Literal Magazine*

THE ANIMAL ON THE ROCK

OTHER BOOKS BY DANIELA TARAZONA AVAILABLE IN ENGLISH
TRANSLATION

Divided Island

The Animal on the Rock

Daniela Tarazona

translated by Lizzie Davis and Kevin Gerry Dunn

Deep Vellum Publishing
Dallas, Texas

Deep Vellum Publishing
3000 Commerce Street, Dallas, Texas 75226
deepvellum.org · @deepvellum

Deep Vellum is a 501c3 nonprofit literary arts organization founded in 2013
with the mission to bring the world into conversation through literature.

Support for this publication has been provided in part by grants from the
National Endowment for the Arts, the Texas Commission on the Arts, the City
of Dallas Office of Arts and Culture, the Communities Foundation of Texas,
and the Addy Foundation.

LIBRARY OF CONGRESS CATALOGING-IN-PUBLICATION DATA

Names: Tarazona, Daniela, 1975- author. | Davis, Lizzie, translator. |
Dunn, Kevin Gerry, translator.
Title: The animal on the rock / Daniela Tarazona ; translated by Lizzie
Davis and Kevin Gerry Dunn.
Other titles: Animal sobre la piedra. English
Description: First English edition. | Dallas, Texas : Deep Vellum
Publishing, 2025.
Identifiers: LCCN 2025009034 (print) | LCCN 2025009035 (ebook) | ISBN
9781646053971 (paperback) | ISBN 9781646053988 (ebook)
Subjects: LCGFT: Novels.
Classification: LCC PQ7298.43.A73 A6513 2025 (print) | LCC PQ7298.43.A73
(ebook) | DDC 863/.7--dc23/eng/20250311
LC record available at https://lccn.loc.gov/2025009034
LC ebook record available at https://lccn.loc.gov/2025009035

Exterior design by Emily Mahon
Interior layout and typesetting by KGT

PRINTED IN THE UNITED STATES OF AMERICA

CONTENTS

"What kind of animal is that?" I asked him, and I instinctively asked this in a gentle tone so as not to wound him with my curiosity. I asked him what kind of animal it was, but the tone in which I asked the question perhaps included: "Why are you doing that? What is it you lack that makes you have to invent a dog? And why not, instead, get a real dog? Given that dogs do exist! Or was putting a collar round its neck the only way of possessing that creature's elegance?"

—Clarice Lispector, "Love,"
from *Too Much of Life*
trans. Margaret Jull Costa and Robin Patterson

His heart was pounding so hard that it even hurt.
—Fyodor Dostoyevsky, *Crime and Punishment*
trans. Richard Pevear and Larissa Volokhonsky

I

Annunciation

My house was the site of an extraordinary event. After my mother's death, a gray cat came into my room and urinated underneath my bed.

It came in while I was packing and looked at me like it knew me. I yelled at it to get out and my heart leapt inside my chest. Its presence compelled me to leave the room. I observed it from the doorway, the cat was calm, but I was trembling. It climbed onto the bed to sniff at my luggage and stayed there, curled up on the mattress, bothered neither by my displeasure nor my theatrics. I went back with a broom to shoo it away, if it hid or remained as it was, I didn't know what I would do. It dove under the bed. There's no getting it out from there, I thought.

It was one in the morning, I paced the living room, frightened by the animal's sturdy corpulence. I saw the kitchen window was open, flowerpots overturned on the ledge, and said aloud, "It came in through there."

The cat meowed from the bedroom. It seemed to be in heat.

(Sometimes the noise of the world makes us howl inside and we contain it.)

The cat paused at my bedroom door to lick its chest. Then it went into the kitchen and escaped.

I know when the city goes still. It happens between three and four in the morning and lasts just a few minutes, the hour when no one's out, the moment of silence.

Since my mother died, nights are all thoughts. I go to bed tired, sleep little, wake trembling. I'm not sick. I want to escape. I long for the strength that will carry me.

I think about trying my luck where my mother was born but then reconsider—I wouldn't feel right there. So I decide to go abroad.

The way out isn't built of articulated thoughts. It's desire in its purest state: running like a chased animal.

When my mother died, her face wasn't a face anymore. Her cheekbones were sunken in her flesh, the oval of her countenance spread, a crown on her hardened body. My mother's mouth was a slice in greenish skin. Before the cremation, I kissed her forehead.

Weeks later, the terrible sharpness of that image has yet to soften.

I'm getting out. The force that urges me on is the opposite of death. I will escape, outpace loss. Today I got out of bed and had to lean against the wall. I have vertigo.

I don't want to inhabit my body. My hands are heavy: the battered claws of an animal that has to fight for its food. My eyes no longer detect the brightness of colors. This afternoon, I heard a voice that wasn't my own inside me. I'm giving over my thoughts to some-one who talks to me but whose face I don't know.

It helps when I imagine going elsewhere might bring relief.

I'll brace myself with the secrets I keep. My flesh, I know, is equipped with powerful attributes—what those are, I'm not sure, but I have observed certain facts: I'm able to adapt, I've deftly survived crises. My body is nimble even if sometimes it acts otherwise. If I want, I can be quick to evade danger. But what I'm describing now is inescapable. I feel my body's weight, its drive is real. I'll reclaim my vitality when I arrive. The changes to my system have already begun.

These spontaneous shifts are now also affecting my mind. I perceive my surroundings differently, and at least once a day, my head spasms like it does before a strong emotion comes on. I'm intrigued by the possibil-ities of this reality. My once-obedient muscles are now lethargic, and in exchange, my extremities are more flexible. If I want, I can twist my arms to fully cup both shoulder blades without any pain or tightness, and I've gone bowlegged, knees leaning to either side.

II

Wrath

I'm going to the airport, I tell the one-eyed woman at the taxi stand.

The car pulls away, and I look at the street to confirm that I'm moving.

Then one hand took another hand. My mouth kissed her forehead. I can't accept defeat. *Death and Transfiguration:* a young girl's hand on a dead woman's forehead. My mother, invincible, dead. The gods die.

In the distance, I see the fence around the airport, the stairs where people watch planes take off and land. Soft drinks in hand, spectators look on as metal occupies air.

I imagine one of them seeing my plane. One of them knowing I fled.

Movement leaves no mark. Forward motion doesn't scar. The surfaces of the streets I know cease to exist for me. I cover my tracks as I walk.

My mother disappeared because her body became smoke.

In the air, sleep comes. I'll be next to a teenager for ten hours. I don't want to talk to anyone. I hope they think I'm mute. Instead of asking for a tomato juice, I'll point to the carton and lift one finger, I'll bring my hands together in supplication, to substitute for my voice.

An animated video tells us what to do in the event of a water landing. The cast: a woman and a little boy, Asian and white, who move like their limbs have springs in them and smile as they simulate an emergency.

Smiling has its place in an emergency. Smiling saves you, a soft denial accepted among humans.

The teenager pulls a device for playing music from her bag, puts the right earbud in, then the left, stretches, is content.

I curl up as much as the seat allows so I can rest.

Air seems different in a plane, it's even lighter, less palpable. "Air is never palpable," I murmur with sleep-swollen eyes.

I do my mute routine with the flight attendant. She looks at me and doesn't know whether to respond in kind or speak. I leave her entangled in her doubt.

The teenager's feet wiggle in her complimentary airline socks.

I know little of outer space. Looking out the window of the plane, I think of black holes. Dimensions are only within the brain's membranes, but we don't realize it. My brain quivers like the brain of any other living thing, and yet, though it unnerves me to acknowledge it: something is growing inside my head. I suppose the operations of my mind are unforeseeable; its patterns can't be predicted because I don't know what I'll live through next. No one knows that.

I cross clouds, swoop down to the right altitude to see: a woman walks along the street near her house; from above she appears even smaller, her movements are lost in distance. She's going to the bank to pay her phone bill. She skirts a park and keeps walking. The woman has no face, or I can't make out her features at this altitude. She stops at the corner of an avenue to cross; the bank is on the other side. She looks around at the pedestrians who, like her, are waiting.

One thing you can see from here: this woman is afraid of the others. Her fear makes her wedge her bag under one arm and cross without noticing the man trying to give her an envelope. The woman doesn't see him, or acts like she doesn't, and keeps walking. He stands there, envelope in hand, not going after her. He attempted but didn't succeed. The woman gets in line. Now I'm close: I notice her temples are throbbing, as if her rising blood pressure is visible. It's Mercedes, my sister.

I didn't realize before, but her hands are young. She's nervous and keeps looking over her shoulder. She turns to the man behind her in line:

"Did you hear what I said to the teller?"

"You said something to the teller?"

My sister makes a dismissive gesture and adds:

"I should have known. You don't get it either."

I wake to a chime in the cabin. The "fasten seat belt" light is on. The flight attendant reinforces it, adding that there may be turbulence due to inclement weather. My seat belt is already fastened; I didn't think to unfasten it. I will get off this plane in one piece.

My sister, Mercedes, used to live somewhere else, but every so often, she would acknowledge that the place didn't exist. Mercedes wanted to keep her insides from decaying. The world as she perceived it consisted entirely of her own tremors.

My mother was deboning a chicken for lunch and didn't stop my sister, though I don't know if she would have anyway.

Mercedes had wanted to die since she was young. I don't care to remember it now that I'm leaving, it doesn't matter anymore if she was ever dead or alive.

After the fall, the world was black like she used to imagine it. Mercedes opened one eye but saw nothing. She felt her body losing its heaviness, her bones growing lighter—she must have smiled, knowing that she would die soon. Delighting in new sensations, she heard sounds she couldn't identify, listened as they pulled at her: the magnetism of air around her lifeless body.

My sister raised birds inside herself that pecked and tore at her guts. That's how she described it to me.

Her suffering inspired me to resist. We have to save our blood.

I'll entrust myself to myself, to my thoughts. In the last few hours, faced with the full force of this new future, I've concluded I'll lose the memories.

I've decided my life will be happy.

Looking out the window, I noticed we were no longer over the ocean. I saw the earth, covered in trees.

III

I Dream of the Jungle

Before boarding the plane, I went days without sleeping. Moving my head made me dizzy, I ate just enough to not starve, and my skin began to itch as if I were sunburned. I had told my friend Felipe what was happening over the phone, but because my mother had died so recently, he thought it was normal. I didn't think my symptoms were side effects of grief. Beyond the pain of accepting that it had come time for my mother to disappear, my body was now strange to me, equipped with a new and inexplicable vitality.

That last month, I'd been astonished to notice my eyes growing slightly larger: I felt a tightness in them

I couldn't describe, like the puffiness they have when you first wake up, but all day.

On my final night at home, an unusual dream strengthened my resolve to get away.

I knew I was incapable of halting the changes to my body—the dream confirmed they were no longer within my control. I was walking low to the ground, dragging myself through a swamp whose stench is lodged in my nostrils. Years earlier, on a trip to the southern jungle, I'd gone to a mangrove where I was struck by the odor of rot emanating from trees and whatever else lived there, all of it trapped in an endless cycle of putrefaction and birth. In the dream I crawled on the ground, through reeds, leaves, and mud. Most puzzling of all, my body was far more agile than usual, or rather, the rhythm of my movements had changed. The trees were immense, so large that I—or what-ever I wanted to be in the dream—couldn't see their crowns; I was tiny relative to the rest. There was a moment when, terrified by my dream and how real it seemed, I nearly woke up. But in half sleep, I distin-guished the illusion, my fears dispersed. I continued to crawl, legs sinking into the boggy ground; I went back to enjoying the jungle scene and listened attentively to its sounds. I stopped when I felt discomfort in one arm, looked at it, shot awake; it wasn't my arm but the arm of another being, a different species of animal.

My mother liked cats. She had nothing new to say about them, just the usual: she'd talk about their agility, their poise, their finesse as they walked among the most fragile items on a shelf. She also liked to leave the door open so they could go out and experience the world, because the cats always came back home, sometimes worse for wear or half starved, but they came back, and my mother would feel proud.

I was describing my dream, but I didn't mention the joy of my time in that jungle—joy from the satisfaction of occupying that space, which felt like somewhere I was once happy.

The fear my own home provoked in me was so deep that I needed to flee. In moments of panic, contours seemed threatening: the corners of furniture, the uneven staircase, the outline of the roof (which was broken as an abstraction): I thought first of the roof, leaned out the front door, and craned my neck to see how high it was. My appraisal wasn't linked to the idea of danger, but it did make me see the roof as a risk. I wasn't thinking of jumping off, it was more that the roof itself represented a threat.

My fear compounded when I thought of Mercedes's illness. If we'd both grown in the same womb, how could we not be alike? Our carnality terrified me. Later, I regained my strength and affirmed my plans out loud, repeating "I'm leaving" over and over, an incantation.

Meanwhile, my body continued revealing strange things to me: I was lither than I used to be, extraordinarily flexible, as confirmed when I swept under the bed (after the cat's visit) and folded nearly in half only to then straighten up with almost no effort. The dizziness, though, was worse in the afternoons, and there were also other afflictions: my hands ached in the mornings, I can only compare it to the few times I've done tedious kitchen tasks, like cleaning shellfish; and my knuckles throbbed, I got in the habit of soaking them in hot saltwater. Days went by, and I came to accept that pain, since it would more or less dissipate once I'd been standing for a few hours.

The weather in the city changed; the thunderstorms were starting.

I think I had to lose consciousness. The alternative was to take off my clothes and stay in bed sleeping all day.

I know I did all the things a person does before traveling; there was enough drive in me to sort out the practical matters: I bought a ticket one afternoon, and that night, I packed a moderately sized suitcase. It wasn't just the cat's visit that made me uneasy that day—washing the knives, I felt like they might cut me, like they had lives of their own. I sat down to breathe and let the thought clear, and abruptly an image came to my mind: the jungle encircling me, a warning from the dream, and I fell asleep.

Now I'm surprised I dared to board the plane. I don't know how I got on a flight so long without overwhelming panic.

The inclement weather has passed. A good time for the lavatory.

On the plane, the passengers sleep.

A tall German-looking man goes in first; I stand by the door and wait.

Something I don't understand is happening to me. I wouldn't have noticed if it weren't so intense. I smelled my urine and it's different than before: it smells sweet.

I eat the piece of chicken the flight attendant brings. It's smothered in viscous sauce. I hope I don't have trouble digesting it, because my digestion has changed, too. My distress must be obstructing my body's natural processes.

On the tray there's a pastry, which I also eat. As I bring it to my mouth, I see the skin of my hand. I look at both my arms, notice how my green T-shirt gives them a similar tone. I have a thought—where it comes from, I don't know—and write it down: "The skin of your limbs, your face, and your stomach will soon be useless to you." The moment I'm done thinking it, my limbs start to itch again; I scratch fiercely and conclude that my nerves are also the cause of the itchiness. I try to sleep a little.

When I wake up, I look at my skin again, notice it's paler, think even its texture has changed.

I pinch myself, rub one hand against the other. My skin has lost sensitivity. My sense of touch is diminished.

The itchiness continues, if I scratch it's worse, but I can't stop.

The teenager wakes up, she's had an enviable nap.

I see the skin detaching itself from certain parts of my arms.

I'll arrive in a place that's right on the ocean. There, along the coast, the abundance of trees thins. The trees stay away from the sea because they can't grow in the sand.

IV

Death

I'm relieved to have reached my destination.

I buy a train ticket at the airport kiosk. I get a coffee.

I must have fallen asleep when I took my seat on the train, because I don't remember when it started moving. My memory conjures the arthritic hands of the elderly woman who sat across from me, they looked like my mother's. She was resting her hands on her stomach when she died.

I lifted her from the bed; she was thin, and in the temperature of her skin, I sensed the nearness of death. She asked me to take her to the bathroom. The last

liquid to leave her body mixed with the toilet's chlo-
rinated water.

In that stream, my mother relinquished some
delicate, vital thing. The medication made her urine
smell like camphor.

Death was inevitable: grief, then. "My mother is
dying; my mother is stuck to white porcelain. What's
left is clawing at that smooth surface, and then she'll
be dead," I shouted at Mercedes, who was adjusting
the bed pillows.

My mother, in her last moments, said she was
floating.

She said other words, made incoherent pronouncements from the land of her brain, which was
starting to dry up; the water was gone and the fish
were dying. My mother gulped mouthfuls of air and
moved her lips slowly. She craved the exhalation she
had been trying to summon for months, she wanted to
die breathing.

When her body emptied—the muscle tone
abruptly diminished—she put her hands on her stomach, pressed her lips together, and when she released

them, Mercedes and I heard a gentle sound: her last expression was a moan.

From the corner of my eye, I watched death flash like a thunderclap: a bolt of silver lightning at the nape of my mother's neck, fearsome in scope and sound.

Within minutes her skin had changed. When the heartbeats stop repeating, the face dehydrates and tinges green.

My sister put one more pillow under her head, covered her, and said three times: "She won't be going anywhere now."

In this new place, only I exist; in my past, only the dead. I've secured a room at a clean guesthouse. I shower and then nap. When I wake up, I stare in disbelief at the outline of my own body on the other side of the bed: a single piece of delicate skin with all my wrinkles and fingerprints; it feels like the glue I used to put on my palms as a child. I gape at the skin, taking off my shirt to examine my torso, not understanding what my eyes detect: I'm swollen; my pores are bigger, or seem to be; and my complexion is a new shade. I look back at the skin, gather it into both hands, feel it. I notice the chickenpox scars on the part that used to cover my forehead. I touch every inch of the skin because I want to remember it clearly. This skin is my history, fully intact. I sloughed it off with careful movements.

I pick up the skin and take it to the trash can in the bathroom. I look at it there, lost forever, and feel like crying because there's no one to tell. My legs shake.

Before falling asleep, I'd wanted to go to the shore. I sit in bed watching TV for an hour then pack my suitcase and bring it with me because I don't know how long I'll be gone.

I'm disoriented. I thought the coast was just north, but I've been walking for two hours and don't know where to go. I don't want to talk to anyone. I dread the idea of making conversation—what could I say?

I'm afraid. A sadness has settled in my throat, and if I speak, I'll cry. Then anyone who hears will ask what's wrong. My mind won't comply, it acts independently—like someone else speaking inside me—and although I'm walking on the street, where real events are taking place, I can't retain them. I'm in a state of sustained confusion.

A moment ago, I thought I was naked, looked at my body, and didn't recognize it.

My skin still itches. I examine my forearms: the swelling has gone down, my pores have shrunk—I think—but in my muscles there's a new heat, which sometimes subsides and turns cool. I scratch at my skin incessantly, even my legs itch now.

An unknown future awaits me, a future like everyone else's but less graceful. Either my wish to escape was in vain, or the exit I took—what's happening to me now—was the only way out left.

V

Rest

I want to scale a rock on the beach, stay there until I need water. I go. I climb onto the rock because it's now the one thing I desire, settle in, and understand this will be my place from now on.

The sun warms me, and my afflictions ease. I notice the skin on my wrists is thickening.

I've come because here, I have both land and water. I can soak in the sea whenever I want and afterward tread on the earth. I need both elements at hand, wouldn't know how to live otherwise.

Shortly after I arrive, exhaustion prevents me from witnessing certain events. I fall asleep.

The witness's role is to verify facts. But the witness's heart doesn't always possess astral qualities, doesn't give off light. Witnesses are often weak, often get carried away by their passions, which then obscure what they see. Much of history comes from their gaze. In a person's own life, in that limbo where a self feels the pulse of its viscera, no one can speak in our name. I offer my testimony knowing that others suffer in this same way but cannot document it.

VI

Witnesses

A man and a dog-like anteater sit down near the rock where I'm sleeping. I watch them through half-open eyes, they're like a mirage.

The man stands up. He's heading back toward the pier. Just then he notices my presence, sees me lying there, sleeping.

They come closer to the rock.

Both stand before me. Look at me. The anteater reaches toward me with his snout, becomes uneasy. He must think I'm dead.

The man takes a step, and the anteater, wanting to leave, pulls him in the opposite direction. The man restrains him: "Wait, Lysander," he says.

I'm coiled up. The man touches my arm and I

don't move; I'd like them to leave. He pats me again and again, wants to be sure I'm not dead.

I open my eyes, and he's captive of my perfectly round irises, the strangest blend of green and red. I rub my eyelids only to find my lashes are gone. The man continues to look at me as if encountering a here-tofore-unknown animal. I try to meet his gaze and he averts it, it rests on the sea. When he turns his head, I take in his profile: the lines of his face are smooth, he barely has any features.

The anteater tugs on his leash, but the man keeps a tight grip and looks back at me. "Do you need some-thing?" he says loudly, assuming I have poor hearing.

I sit up slowly, listlessly; my body aches. I look at the ground, now avoiding his eyes, and tell him I'm hungry.

My feebleness can't be ignored: I can barely stand on my feet. I falter near the man as if my legs no longer answer to me; it's minutes before I manage to get up. The anteater takes an interest, nudging my legs with his snout; I push him back so he'll stay away. He scares me.

—

We walk. The man moves along as best he can: he has the anteater's leash in his left hand and his right arm around my shoulders, clutching me to his body.

When we get to his house, I wait leaning against the wall while he finds his keys and opens the door. We enter. Lysander goes to the kitchen for water, and the man takes me to the sofa. He gives me a small blanket I wrap myself in.

He pulls over a chair and sits down. He talks, asks my name and where I'm from. I don't respond. He gets up to look for a towel. When he comes back and hands it to me, I'm in the same position, but shaking.

I set the towel down on the sofa. He shows me the door to the bathroom.

Lysander comes back, a bit calmer than before. Later, when he's done circling me, I give him a smile, brief and small.

The man has become my companion.

He says he's grown used to Lysander, though the neighbors still find him strange. Lysander is part of his life. He was alone until he found him.

The man wants to trim Lysander's nails because they're too long, Lysander suffers the fate of apartment-bound dogs: without earth to scrape his nails against, he grows talons that can only be cut with garden shears.

He tells me Lysander has developed respiratory problems, since this isn't his natural habitat; the man feels like it's his fault. When he's not well, Lysander lets his tail droop but keeps his long snout raised in a dignified manner.

The day they found me, my companion had told Lysander that a walk along the shore might do him good, and the animal had looked at him with moist eyes, as if knowing that this particular walk would be different. He had put up a fight, which was strange, since usually he's so docile. The man told me it was hard, that at points he had to drag along the animal.

My companion had gone out to see the reddening sky: "The most spectacular sunset this autumn," he remembered—but of course that was a trick, the pure naiveté of sight.

When he goes out to walk with Lysander, he knows he'll be under less scrutiny. He says people judge him for the smallness of his features but seem to be less puzzled when they encounter him with his strange pet.

VII

My Virtue

On my sixth night in this house, my companion says he's going to bed and that I should knock if I need anything. He calls Lysander over and slowly closes the door, not taking his eyes off me. I've realized I can see the ocean through the window, and I stare at it until it makes me sleepy.

I told him I'm sick but it's the opposite. My body knows this is the start of an evolutionary cycle. I haven't been brave enough to discuss it with him—our conversations are disjointed and he barely understands what I'm going through. Now that I know a little of his story, I can see why he looks at me with distrust, but, by the end of my sentences, always believes me and nods. He says he has been happy, but anyone who passes him and Lysander on the street would know right away that he's suffered. I like Lysander, though I never thought I'd sleep soundly at night with an animal like him near me.

Nothing I ever imagined resembles what I'm now living: if I think back on the passage of earlier days, their predictable cadence, I might even conclude I was born overnight, from a body that wasn't my mother's.

The swelling of my features has gone down, and I'm left with new capabilities: when I close my eyes, I can still see the shapes of things, my eyelids are translucent. These new virtues sharpen with each day. I'm less vulnerable to heat, and previous anxieties—like people's voices in small spaces—have lost their relevance. I feel calmer, except at night, when my skin becomes so sensitive the bedsheets burn.

Once the sun has set, moving at all becomes a challenge, my limbs weigh me down.

The skin over my joints is even thicker, and I know

my scent has changed. Lysander approaches me with familiarity. His movements suggest he knows me. It's true I feel more animal now than when I arrived.

We leave the house.

I tell my companion: "Seeing the ocean gives me hope. The water can't disappear because if it did, we would die on the spot. Besides, I've always thought of myself as amphibian. What are you?" He's silent for a moment, then says: "I'm going to disappear. I'm not saying death will take me, just that one day I'll disappear, possibly to go and live someplace else."

An older man walks past, stops, brazenly stares, then settles his eyes upon Lysander and says, "We're on the brink of collapse." My friend looks at his feet, he's furious but controls himself. I think our appearance scares people. I've lost a lot of weight and my

skin is a new color; my companion is hardly graceful and has a restless look in his eyes; and Lysander,
for his part, incites anger almost everywhere he goes.
People seem offended when they see we're keeping
an anteater as a pet. My companion considers him
a domesticated animal, but maybe that's what so
offends them: the idea of keeping such a thoroughly
undomestic creature as a pet. I'm the same: a woman
belonging to him, but of another species.

VIII

Orifice

The moment of greatest alarm has arrived: I've lost my sex organs. Like my joints, my genitals are now covered with thicker skin.

When I decided to tell my companion, he was sitting with his hands interlaced over his knees. He replied that we couldn't go to the doctor or we would become an unsolvable case. Then, after a moment of inspiration, he went on: "What's happening to you could be the product of your mind. I'm impressionable, so if you show me your genitals, I'll see the same thing you do." We sat in silence for half an hour.

He asked, "When you arrived here, did being near water bring you relief? Does sunlight satisfy you? I think I know what you are, it's coming together."

I tried to get him to tell me what he was think-ing; he finally spoke: "You're a mutation, you just didn't realize it. You'll be a different animal before you reach maturity." He asked about my symptoms like a specialist, I answered many of his questions with a *yes*.

I told him that after taking a nap in the guesthouse when I arrived, I woke up with new skin, the empty outline of my body beside the bed.

"I shed my skin like a snake."

"But you're not a snake."

"What am I, then?"

"An iguana or a lizard. Look at your pupils."

"What about between my legs? Everything's gone."

"It isn't gone, it's just different. You have an ori-fice, don't you?"

"Yes. I'm going to be a reptile."

I'm confused. If I try to process this transformation with rational tools, I lose hope. Nothing I know is of use in facing this phenomenon. But my companion has more compassion for me than I do: he has accepted his role as witness to my metamorphosis.

Lysander, too, shows great care for me. He licks my neck when I wake up and puts his snout where I can pet it, but only a little. Then he leaves, suddenly arrogant. Lysander is a proud creature. It's possible he wonders about the position he finds himself in. Maybe when he's alone and it's quiet, before he falls asleep, he has animal memories—former adventures, his freedom—and finds them troubling. But his normalcy lies in the rightness of his body. He uses his body, knows it's alive and can manage his circumstances, that's where his pride comes from.

I, like Lysander, am inoffensive to my companion.

I'm breathing in a new way. My rib cage doesn't balloon like before and its rhythms have changed. My throat palpitates, so does my tongue, in sync with the air that enters my body.

My companion applies a special wax to my skin. He

says I seem to need moisturizing, that this skin hasn't adjusted to captivity; it's used to being in the jungle, under the sun.

I was aroused by his touch. My skin changed color, it became pink, and I embraced my companion, latching onto his back. I wanted to have him. An erroneous thought passed through my mind: bite his chest, devour his flesh. He stayed calm, didn't object to the strength of my arms, just said he would give in if I released him. I did. My companion held my head in his hands, told me I was the most beautiful woman. The impulse lessened and I could control it. To bite him would be to accept my animality all at once—it was better to wait.

Shortly after, I had my first paralysis. Though I tried, I couldn't move my head. It was as if an external force had obliged me to remain rigid, eyes fixed on a corner of the room. My companion wasn't alarmed; he made an observation: "You're a prehistoric animal, and you're watching the passage of time in a way that no one else can."

We go swimming. My companion and I get in. Lysander stays with our clothes.

I'm underwater doing clumsy, dangerous flips. My movements are better coordinated on land, in the water I have no mastery over my body. There's a barrier reef out in front of this beach, so the waves are gentle, I'm only a little scared.

I look at my hands. Between the skin of them and my eyes is the water that highlights my limitations. Down below I'm whiter, I look healthy, my fingers are thicker. Now I look at my belly, note my underwear detaching from my skin, its coverage all for show. I stand on my knees from time to time, tired of being suspended in this new environment. The stones at the bottom, erstwhile shells, have left marks on my knees. I dunk my head again—later my companion said I looked like an old woman bathing with care—and try to discern the roar of the sea, then confirm a well-known fact: the sounds of water are from another kingdom; the music is distorted, the notes, lower. I bring my head back to the surface, look toward the beach and search for Lysander, and notice the current has dragged me leftward, a natural occurrence I find startling; I spot my companion swimming in the distance. I didn't move, nor did I notice myself being dragged, but I'm at the water's mercy.

Now I want to go belly-up, I struggle to lean back, I float, floating is an extraordinary event. If you think about it, floating seems impossible. One thing doesn't become another simply because they are paired. Flesh isn't like water. I don't understand how they coexist: the air and the plane I arrived on, the water on the earth.

I look at the sky. The clouds run swiftly, the midday sun does me good. A fish swims by, flaunting its innate aquatic ability. The fish knows I'm here and avoids my legs, recognizing me.

I take half my body out of the water and stay that way a while, watching the salt appear on my collarbone as I dry. I run a finger over the marks and bring it to my mouth, taste it.

I consider leaving the sea. I decide to get out, but first I'll dive and try to cling to the seabed with my whole body. I succeed, reach the sand, lie down, notice how small my lungs are, I don't have the air reserves to play at being a fish. Rising to my knees is all it takes to reach the surface. I crawl toward the beach, the water goes one direction and I go the other, then the forces reach equilibrium.

When I leave the water and nothing is left but damp sand—it soaks up the liquid pressed into it by the force of my feet on the ground—I feel a bite on my right heel. It hurts. The salt on my skin enters the wound; in the sand, I see the withdrawing pincer of a crab whose body is hidden. The wound bleeds.

I go toward Lysander. My companion stays in the water. As when I arrived, I yearn to climb onto a rock. Nearby there are some white slabs. I tell Lysander I'm going over there, lift my arm and point in that direction.

I lie on my stomach on one of the slabs. Satisfied, I could die now, I think. My pulse gradually slows. The heat feels good on my skin. I touch my orifice, try to find what I used to feel, but I'm not able to. The rays of the sun are drying me, the rock is hot, then I think of how before my mother died, I wanted a child—before my mother died, I had been living with a man who wanted children—I remember that desire and feel immediate disappointment.

I lift my head and look for my companion. He's getting out of the water.

I return to my thoughts.

If I'm going to be a reptile, I imagine I'll have to mate the reptilian way, though I don't know what that way is. When the heat of the sun has taken all my body, something paralyzes me fully. I am, again, catatonic, immobile; I try to break free but I can't. The paralysis doesn't frighten me. I accept this new pattern along with everything else.

My companion sits down next to me. He saw me swimming, he says: "Some frogs float belly-up and play dead so they won't be hunted, others fold their legs and change how they look so their predators can't see where they're vulnerable."

I don't say anything because I can't in my current state. Maybe my instincts can sense that I'm in danger.

He turns his back to me, but I see he's begun to masturbate. He does it for several minutes, increasing the force and the speed of his hand. He gets up, leaving a streak of semen behind.

Instinct prompts me to sit on top of it, naked, and press my new genitalia against that semen-stained sand.

IX

My Name

My companion tells me I was asleep for two months. He looks me in the eyes, then looks away.

I bring one hand out from under the sheets to scratch my face then stare at my arm with astonishment: sharp little points like thorns have begun to grow there. Inside me, I sense a new and pleasant temperature, a slight coolness. There are other things I want to explain; for example, the certainty that my viscera exist: I can feel my insides. My intestines are grazing the walls of my abdomen, my heart is sitting softly atop my lungs. I never imagined this, never thought my condition would bring these sensations.

My companion, too, confirms something real is happening to me, says he spent hours sitting on my bed during my long sleep, noting the changes one by one. "Your skin changed every day," he says.

In addition, I feel something developing inside me, but I can't see it. What's growing is immaterial, or at least reflects the principle of immateriality. I can compare it to the uncertain moment when the texture of fabric revives the memory of some older sensation.

I know whatever it is that's developing is going to make itself known.

Lysander comes to sit next to my bed, but first examines a hole in the baseboard; he's hungry. On the floor, a new string of ants walks toward the door then loops back. Lysander sticks out his impressive tongue and eats some but also leaves many alive, so as not to deplete the riches. He's an animal who knows.

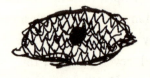 

Tonight, my companion is uneasy in my presence. He doesn't know what to do with me. I think that first image of my face—that naked eye looking at him through the darkness—filled him with an emotion he couldn't name. My gaze reminds him of some unidentifiable experience.

I wake with the sun. It's the end of winter and dawn comes at six thirty in the morning. Lysander is asleep and stays that way a while longer. My companion is uncovered; with the changing season he tossed through the night and pushed the worn-out blanket to the floor. He's wearing a green shirt.

I see the blackened soles of my feet. I'm going to bathe.

My companion sleeps with his mouth open, as if his nose is congested.

I hear him cough and look in. He doesn't move when he sees me. It's like he's mastered the transition from sleep to wakefulness, and nothing can surprise him. When he gets up, I notice a small cloth bag hanging around his neck.

I prepare breakfast, though I have to open every drawer and cupboard to find the bread I'll put in the toaster.

I'll describe the changes I've experienced in detail. As I said, there's more skin around my joints now, my knees have fully vanished beneath flesh. Or, the skin over them has grown so thick I can no longer tell where bones meet. Over the course of months, that new, multiplied skin has become so elastic that I can fold it, and there's even a wrinkle on the underside of my leg, a trace of recent movements.

My mutation is nothing special, all mutating animals debut qualities. The same goes for me.

When I was a child, on sleepless nights, I would stealthily close the door to my room—my mother made me keep it open—and find relief imagining a scene: me, confined to a hospital bed, my mother and sister drawing near to stroke my hair and comfort me. I knew I was going to die, what I had was terminal. I'd lull myself to sleep by envisioning my own death.

Maybe I'll wake up one day in a shell: me, inside an egg, about to be born. Maybe my family was a strange species and I never knew it.

Now I have the photo of my sister. I look at her carefully, as I never have before. My sister was stunning, her beauty transfixes me, but something breaks the effect: my sister has the same mole as me, that brown spot on her right leg, which she never mentioned, or which I forgot. I look at the picture again and find another anomaly of my memory, or worse, something I never knew about her life: she's wearing a bandage around one knee and hiding her right hand behind her back. I look for more clues or similarities in the album and find the photo that always made me uneasy: my sister's right hand—which she's trying to shield from the photograph—peeking through the folds of a quilt: her hand and face are different colors. There it is: my sister was turning into something else and wanted to stop.

Two days ago, we went for a swim in the ocean. Since then, my companion has been smiling more. I lent him my notebook so he could write about how I told him my name. We're getting used to each other.

Me Hama Irma

He spends the days consumed by my transformation, frequently reading the used biology textbooks he finds at a local bookstore. The other day, he joked that I should be happy if I'm a newt, because their average lifespan is fifteen years.

My companion had a beautiful childhood. I can tell from what I see: the proportions of his back, the thickness of his neck. I've looked at pictures of him; the one I liked best is of him and two friends, a low-angle shot framing their torsos, and behind them, a church bell tower.

—

In some places, the spikes on my arms have grown into more sizeable protrusions covered in scales; I think in a few days the same will happen on my legs. I have a sense of the order of these alterations, though I don't know where it comes from.

I heard a voice say it was there to explain something that happened without my realizing it. It told me I'm pregnant. I followed my instincts correctly that day on the beach: it was right that I sat on the streak of semen. My species, then, has dispensed with copulation. We're beings who have dwelled on the planet for thousands of years, and our survival instinct is innate. With copulation impossible, we turn to insemination. That's what I did, and rightly. My new sex organs are operational. How will something be born from me? To give life is a desire not influenced by thought, but mandated by the patterns of my species.

If I am turning into a reptile, will my progeny be oviparous?

A few hours ago, my companion tried to dispel that mental lacuna. He said that after he found me on the beach, I talked about my train journey. That when I arrived, I'd been admitted to a hospital; my wrist was still sticky from tape that held the IV in place. I don't remember this.

X

Animality

I look at myself in the mirror. I pause at my pupils, now vertical ovals; the irises have reddened, and in the right eye is a yellow spot that was brown in my prior condition. My ears are at most one-quarter their former size. I look more closely: I don't have moles, they disappeared beneath the greenish veil of my new skin.

Lysander has been aggressive today: he circles me, and when I get close, he rebuffs me with a growl. He doesn't have teeth, but he doesn't need them, his tongue is enough. My companion says Lysander senses my new animality. I've decided to ignore him.

—

At night, my heartbeats are more spaced out. If I think like what I was, if I think from the body of a woman, I get scared and worry I might die, that my heart might stop. During the day it normalizes and maintains a consistent rhythm.

Every day around noon, I go to the beach and lie on a hot rock. I need it, my scales brighten when I do it, and the pain in my joints subsides; the sun gives me comfort. The temperature outside calibrates the temperature of my body, and I know I am immortal when I'm on a rock.

My companion thinks it's dangerous, that I'll hurt myself if the rocks get too hot; we fought, I talked back and didn't care what tone I used, I argued that I'm learning and have to follow my instincts.

My sense of smell has sharpened, and I've noticed I can also smell through my mouth if it's open. I discovered something else after eating: I ran my tongue over the roof of my mouth because it hurt and found two small protrusions there, lined up symmetrically.

Lysander and I have begun competing for food. I didn't expect this to be an issue, the difference between us is clear, but Lysander eats ants, and I've started to enjoy insects, house spiders, mosquitos. Lysander growls when I sniff around in the corners, but I don't intend to stop.

XI

What I Forgot

The door opens; I wake up. A woman in white stands over me saying my name.

I want to know where I am, want the woman to give me details. I ask, but she doesn't respond.

I'm naked under the hospital gown. Someone took off my underwear, and whoever it was also stole my semanario ring. I have long nails, and they're thicker than before; each root has extended almost to each finger's middle phalanx. I smell meat. I'm what smells of it, of living flesh like a chicken's, the sweat of a kept animal. But I'm not a bird.

The woman takes my wrist and looks at her watch then pats me twice on the shoulder and says I'm improving. She has long nails, too, except hers are painted an elegant scarlet red.

I ask her again what's happening, and she answers that she's not authorized to discuss it, that the doctor on call will tell me. I don't have my own doctor, either, just whoever's been assigned the anonymous stretchers like mine for the night.

I start to cry like a little girl. The nurse hands me a handkerchief from the table beside the bed. I'm not sad but something internal brings me to tears.

My hospital room is pleasant.

The nurse checks the IV, glances at an electric apparatus by my side, and says she'll be back.

A doctor comes that night. He tells me my recovery is miraculous, and that except for my hand and foot deformities, I can think of myself as a normal woman (he smiles like he's nervous when he says this). He gives me sleeping pills. When I wake up, my backside aches. I lift my gown and see bruises where the syringe pierced my skin.

I get up, open the closet door, find my suitcase. I dress, wash my face, and, before leaving, make sure there are no witnesses in the hallway. The suitcase is hard to carry: my claws snag on the handle. My head hurts: I blame the drugs they gave me.

I go outside, the sun is beginning its descent. I put my hands in my jacket pockets to avoid startling anyone.

Walking north, I let my sense of smell and the wind lead me. To the north is the coast, and that's where I want to go.

I sleep under the eaves of a flower shop, fondly recalling the nurse's soft hands. I don't think I'll ever know why I woke up there. The voice returns, affirming the resilience of my spirit. It spoke an inner truth that gave me the will to find my companion.

My transformation brings strength; when it's complete, nothing on earth will be capable of affecting me. My line will survive forever, or at least go unbroken for a vast and unimaginable length of time. My mother, my sister, and I will have descendants.

The next morning, the florist rouses me with a kick. It's not a sharp kick, just enough force to bring me to my senses without too much of a scare. I tell him I'll leave shortly, I just need to gather myself, put on my shoes. I ask for water so I can wash my face. The man, whose jowls have begun to sag from age, says he'll let me use the bathroom.

I enter the flower shop. The arrangements are unattractive: too many simulations of a nature that doesn't exist. Not a single bouquet with any wildness in it. The bathroom at the back of the shop is dark; under the narrow sink, a bucket on the verge of over-flowing catches the drip from the pipe on the ceiling. An irreparable drip, I guess.

I wash my face, careful not to scratch myself. I stick out my tongue at the mirror and see another undeniable sign of my transformation: on the left side, my tongue is thicker, and its back half has changed, too, into smooth and grayish flesh.

On my way to the coast, I encounter a man without legs who asks for spare change. I give him the only coin I have on me. The man didn't lose them in an accident; there are no scars on the skin that sticks out of his pantlegs.

If I didn't have legs, I'd drag myself along. With help I could tend to my daily needs. I have no one. I'll appreciate my legs, then. Incomprehensible nature has been generous with me, though it'd be easy to think the opposite. Far from diminishing the powers inherent to my body, nature has chosen to endow me with new talents. Taking one step, then another, I silently give thanks for its benevolence.

The wind pushes the clouds, and the sun shines with greater intensity. I look straight at it without fearing that its radiance will blind me. When I look away, an image I see and feel takes shape in the center of my forehead—an explosion, a cacophony that makes me stop moving and deafens me for a few minutes; I'm sure that if someone is watching, they'll notice the millions of photons swarming me.

Later on, tormented by a migraine, I understand that the previous pains in my head—the spasms I'd been suffering—were precursors to this eruption. Again, I accept that all I see is mysteriously formed there, shocked into silence before nature.

If along the way I had wanted to speak with anyone on the street, my voice wouldn't have been audible. My tongue, which had grown larger even on that journey, was rigid, and for a time, maybe for hours, I couldn't move it. When night fell, I realized I could control it again. But even so, if I were to find someone who inspired my trust, what would I tell them? My muteness is necessary or unavoidable because what I'm experiencing can only be heard by those disposed to listen. Conversations with others may be the one thing I miss.

I'm composed of fragments, I'm not one complete animal, and from that place of deficiency, I seem strange to those who are.

XII

The Cave

I remembered the train ride. Perhaps the change in latitude, along with my fragile emotional state, made me forget until now.

My neck was stiff. The thrill of being far from home was so intense that my body had gone rigid with adrenaline. But discomfort soon overpowered the joy.

I lifted my head and became extremely dizzy. I got up for the bathroom and walked across the train car, pausing at each seatback within reach; movement heightened my nausea.

I wanted to get off, wanted the train to stop immediately, but we were going through a tunnel. I sat on the toilet, leaned my head against the wall, and allowed myself to be shaken, my head striking the wall again and again. If the train were to stop and I could get off wherever we happened to be, my state would remain unchanged. Rather than subsiding, the shifts in my energy might become more acute. The only way to avoid this kind of moment would be to vanish from the world. Still, knowing I'd left the space I had been in gave me some satisfaction. I recovered by a barely perceptible degree, and with that narrow band of strength, I returned to my seat.

Eyes open, I grew delirious. I saw my sister sitting in a chair, inside a large room with no other objects. My sister had her hands clasped, as if there were something inside them. She couldn't see me, but she knew I was watching her from afar, and she heard my voice.

"Mercedes, you still haven't left."

"I'm waiting for the one love I had to come and say goodbye."

"But he's dead already, Mercedes."

"You don't know anything. The dead don't leave the world. There are dead that walk alongside us, we just don't sense them."

"Are you going to give him whatever you have in your hands?"

"No. What I'm holding is for you."

I came closer, stood right in front of her. Gray hairs flecked Mercedes's brown curls. She had aged. She was sitting like she always did: feet aligned, together, knees also touching, maintaining a forced corporeal symmetry.

My sister extended her hand and said:

"Let me see your right palm."

I held out my hand, wondering what she would give me. She unclasped hers, and I saw the secret. Mercedes looked me in the eyes and said: "This is a piece of my heart. I treated it so it won't spoil, you can store it in a cool, dark place, out of direct sunlight. A wooden box will do."

The fragment of Mercedes's heart seemed to have the texture of a crystal, but when I squeezed it between my index finger and thumb, the crystal was flexible. It looked like a red pearl but larger.

111

—

Then I fell into a well so narrow I could barely pass through it. The wall scraped my knees. I was going away, there was no light in any direction, I managed to look up and saw the darkness I was falling from; downward, everything was the same except my legs were shimmering, I could only conclude that I had acquired a light of my own, phosphorescent.

I was motionless even though now I'm talking of motion. I was unconscious even though now I'm describing what happened. I lived through a moment of collapse. Then the dizziness went away, and with it, any possibility of feeling pain.

I looked out the window. The train stopped. For my own safety, I feigned calm. The people around me wanted lucid phrases. They wanted to know they were traveling with someone normal.

I opened my bag and dug around inside. The elderly woman with arthritic hands wasn't across from me anymore. I was trying to find the mints I'd brought along, feeling for them at the bottom of my bag, still looking out the window: two women were embracing two men on the platform. My hands came up against something solid. From the bag, I extracted a small wooden box I'd never seen before. On its lid was a minuscule bouquet of dried flowers trapped in clear varnish. I opened it and saw without understanding: resting on red velvet, there was something like a pearl, but pink. A living pearl that appeared to be throbbing. An electric shock rose from my abdomen and caused my stomach to cramp. The cramp was so severe that I vomited. I leaned down and vomited something I couldn't identify onto the plastic tray table.

It's possible that the amorous vision I had—a man carrying me to bed in his arms, my knees pressed into his hips—wasn't vision but fact: the man from the train who carried me to the ambulance.

XIII

Another Lost Memory

The florist had given me a light-blue sweater with buttons down the front. I put it on. I was enjoying the walk: the people in that place, at that hour—morning—were happy.

I felt happy too. I had shaken the bad dream I had on the train and was lucid again. I felt grateful to myself, because despite all the difficulties, I had reached this destination.

A sharp pain on my scalp faded to tingling. I scratched and noticed a bump on top of my head that felt like a bone under skin. Am I growing a horn? I wondered. I slid back my hand a bit, felt around on my skull, and was excited to find several bones had emerged in a perfect line. It's the crown of a prehistoric animal, I thought.

I looked at the sky, spotted an eagle flying there, and felt an insurmountable, irrational fear. I went into a phone booth and waited for the terrifying animal to leave.

The subway passed underfoot and rattled my hiding place. My sense of danger increased, and with it, my panic. I decided to leave, but not without first confirming the eagle had gone.

I saw a narrow, quiet street, a dirty street where I could hide. I lay down on the ground; my clothing wasn't too bright, and my gray skin could be mistaken for pavement. There, I felt safe.

A few minutes later, something new in my body caught my attention. At first, I thought it was the trash piled high on the street, masses of bags that sweat in the sun, but then I realized the fetid odor was coming from my own skin. I raised my wrinkled forearm to my nose and inhaled deeply. The stench stayed fixed in my nostrils—the smell of a dead animal. My camouflage was perfect. No predator would come close if I smelled like rotting flesh.

After the terror of the eagle, an hour must have passed before I could go on. My heart was beating slowly, since the sun had reached its zenith. Then I saw the man without legs: he was riding in a wheelbarrow, pushed along by a young man who resembled him. The man without legs looked at me like he knew me, his expression made me uneasy; after the wheelbarrow passed, he kept looking, leaning out around whoever was pushing him. That man frightened me too.

I was close to the place I'd imagined: a cliff overlooking a narrow beach with a rising tide so unpredictable no one visited. People who researched the sea hadn't managed to work out why the water behaved in that way. Maybe the earth was sinking, but no one would ever be able to say, for fear of alarming the locals.

There are things men don't talk about because they're incomprehensible, and worse, they would lead to fatal despair. We must at least believe in the permanence of natural phenomena, even if mutation is their constant.

The beach was deserted. I leaned my head back to admire the height of that wall. The sea made the sound of a beast, the sound of the earth's entrails. The sea comes, the land hisses, draws a sulfurous breath, and then recovers.

The wind made me shiver. I put on the first shirt I found in my suitcase, underneath the blue sweater.

At the far side of the beach, I discovered a small cave in the base of the rock wall. I went inside, put my things on the ground, and felt the fatigue of the journey in my feet. I lay down, arranged my bag like a pillow, and repositioned the wooden box. I felt uncomfortable resting my head on it.

There are days when my thoughts are ordered and flow neatly, moments when I recognize my natural relationship to things. Even so, I've doubted their veracity for a while now. My companion said he could see my uncertainty; he said it was counterproductive for me to despair when I couldn't remember the events of the previous day.

I no longer know if what I've written in these pages is accurate. When I reread them, I find prior mention of my amnesia after the train ride. How could I recover the memory of an event I don't think I lived? Yesterday, in a trance-like state, summoning what human qualities I have left, I tried to piece my past life back together, writing down what I remembered about my arrival at the hospital.

—

The question: If the doctor really examined me, as he said he did, why wasn't he shocked by what he found?

I think I met my companion after I slept in the cave.

I woke up thirsty. I remembered a man and an animal like an anteater had taken me to their home.

That man is now my companion. The animal is an anteater, I said it before, but I'll repeat it to better explain myself. My companion is blond. The anteater has black hair and two gray stripes that extend along either side of his head. He has blond hairs, too, all over his huge body, from his snout to his bristling black tail. The hairs on Lysander's tail are always standing on end, they must grow that way.

I get cold in the afternoon, and I need more sun than I used to. I'm more and more attracted to the sun.

Since I arrived at this house, which I now con-sider mine, or ours—my companion's, Lysander's, and mine—I haven't released that fetid odor again. I'm glad it hasn't happened, I'd be embarrassed if my companion smelled me in that state.

My crest is larger now. The spines that will give me absolute distinction are emerging. My hair from before hasn't fallen out, but it has changed color slightly; it's lighter now, as if the pigmentation in my capillary cells is changing too.

When I go out, I wear a straw hat to fool everyone. And to undermine their certainty: I'm not what they see.

XIV

Home

My companion and I go out to look for firewood. The cold has arrived, and it's worse at night. Lysander doesn't want to come along; he suffers more than we do with falling temperatures.

My companion says someone in town might sell us a bundle. We go to look for such a person, knock on the doors of five houses where my companion always had luck before, but this evening, the neighbors are colder than usual, and their survival instincts curb their generosity.

We pass a house where an old woman stands in her doorway. Her door is the old-fashioned kind, with an upper and lower panel that open independently; she has the lower panel closed and the top one fully open, so we only see half her body. She asks us what we're looking for. "Wood," my companion says. She says her brother will help us.

My companion goes to get wood from the shed with the brother. I stay with the old woman in her living room, worried I'll be left behind there. She shows me a dollhouse she made out of garbage. The furniture is old milk cartons and the walls are aluminum, flattened tin cans, I guess.

My companion comes back with the wood and we say goodbye. Walking away, we glance back every so often, still smiling.

My companion said the man wouldn't take money for the wood. It didn't surprise me, because my new state could also accept that in this same world, there are men who willingly part with their resources.

Tonight my companion bit me in his sleep. I think he was dreaming about some danger, slipped and mistook me for the antagonist. He bit my shoulder and I woke up in a rage. My mouth immediately flooded with a creamy substance; the first time I secreted venom. I almost spewed it at my companion, but some intuition led me to discharge it into an empty glass instead. After I rid myself of the venom, a sweet taste lingered in my mouth. I watched my companion sleep and knew I wanted to care for him until he died.

The night I accepted that I was a quadruped, something happened in the sea. Things are always happening in the sea—that's what my companion said, and
he was right—but what I want to write so I can better
understand it is that when I saw the sea and the sand,
I grasped my destiny.

At daybreak we were frightened, I held tight to my
companion, who also trembled. We heard the people
on the street saying a storm was coming.

What happened was more violent than bad weather.
The rage of men was in the air, and the wind would
bring down their constructions.

When we awoke, though we'd slept just a few hours,
I stopped short of looking out the window, fearing the

spectacle I would see. Later, when the rain stopped, we went out to look up close. The sea had risen and now it was closer to the earth, the roofs of the small houses along the shore barely peeked out above the water, I calculated that at least two city blocks had been submerged.

The algae that covered the streets where we could still walk were of different species, but they had settled on top of each other, into a dense monochrome patch drying in the sunlight. The sun was doing little to cheer the curious few who had come out to behold the phenomenon. Amid the algae, a few fish were dying, and we also saw a black octopus that made me intensely uncomfortable.

The storm revealed the meaning of my mutation. Nature doesn't err; whatever it manifests is a sign of adaptation. Something of that magnitude was bound to strike this coast. My companion agreed. He has lived here for ten years and knows. There's no escaping the variability of events. No force in the universe can halt that. Like this coastline, I had to shed my former attributes. My mutation was driven not just by chance—or conditions I've proven incapable of predicting—but also by my origins. My mother and sister showed the same symptoms. That's my line, though I've managed to flee. I am alive. I will achieve consecration through my actions. That's why I'm pregnant—I want to ensure descendants, reproduce.

Lines cross from one side of my belly to the other, like the wrinkles on my limbs but deeper.

When I woke up under the bed on my four extremities, I tried to stand, but my back feet couldn't support the weight of my body. I accepted it.

I went out to the living room, my companion was awake and eating breakfast, I heard his sounds in the kitchen. I called to him, noticed that my voice was more nasal now, he walked over and found me on the ground. He crouched to see what I was doing, kissed me on the cheek, and said, "Welcome to the world."

Cells copy what the other cells do. It's similar to what I observed in the sea. The body alongside the water floats because it's in water. It's possible that my cells are obeying the stronger ones.

Writing is getting difficult.

My companion is, at this moment, helping me write, I'm dictating because I'm tired and can't continue, not now that I've descended to all fours. I tried to write in bed, lying on my stomach, but I can't. With my front limbs, I can scale rock walls—I did this yesterday—but I can't complete tasks that require precision.

Lysander walks alongside us. Recently, my companion has been amused when he sees us together, because I wrap myself around Lysander's legs while he looks at me, frozen, as if I'm a dangerous animal. Maybe one of my ancestors preyed on his grandparents. But I still see myself in his eyes.

There are new developments, auditory talents I hadn't discovered. When I encircle Lysander's legs, I hear the sound of falling water. I told my companion I've dubbed that moment "the fate of the fountain"; I enjoy it, but I'm not always able to hear it. I just tried to trigger the noise, but I wasn't able to. Instead, I felt—with enormous bewilderment—that a stream of cold water was coming out of my navel. I tried to confirm with my eyes only to realize that I'd imagined it. My navel was dry, it looked the same as always: small, oblong, a scar of necessity. I don't want my navel to disappear, but there's a part of me that can't resist the idea—it's the clearest sign of my past. My companion says he has never seen a reptile with a belly button. As if he's calling my entire mutation into question.

To defend myself, I tell him about the hypothesis I came up with after sensing water in my navel, I tell him it's a sign of something coming to an end. "I didn't realize before," I add, "but my human soul is most likely liquid or transparent phlegm, and it has decided to vacate my body. It's already in transit to an order outside of reason or language."

My companion's response scared me: he said that if I lost my human soul, my language would go extinct next, and my mind would only formulate desert or jungle scenes, depending on where I was. And if that were to happen, I'd never finish this testimony.

There's nothing left now except to give in. My well-being depends on the walks I take with my companion and Lysander. I've lost my self-sufficiency, or at least I lack my former abilities. I can no longer call myself human. I take my adaptation in stride, it doesn't sadden me to think I'll cease being a person, but the changes in my body are happening faster than I can develop my species' faculties.

I'm equipped with unique aptitudes. The tail I began to grow a few days ago has uses I've yet to master.

We spent all day at the beach. I had an episode that surprised me. A group of young people lit a bonfire at dusk and left it burning. I approached and was paralyzed there, astonished by how it consumed the branches, the crackling sound of the wood. The flames were beautiful as they rose high, pointing at the sky through the darkness. I didn't want the blaze to end, if I had been able to, I would have stoked the fire so the flames would never cease.

Between then and now, I've experienced plenitude. I hadn't known fire for what it is, I was ignorant of its benefits. I knew it gave off heat, but not like that; the fire, like me, was the product of incomprehensible recombinations—it emerged from smallness, grew tall, it was the first of all things.

I know we come from materials that burn. I forgot that in my human life; now I've recovered it. I belong to a species whose faculties complement fire. I've confirmed my skin's resistance to heat, and felt the goodness of the sun on my contours; drought has won over my skin; I'll never sweat again. I'm made for this, like an animal from the beginning of time: I find that I'm perfect and right, I was made to become what I am.

Lysander inhaled scraps he shouldn't have: the scales I abruptly cast off, those bits of skin that look like fish scales but thicker, which scattered across the floor of the house.

He's hungrier than usual, but he can't find any ants. The house isn't humid enough, and my companion sweeps every day. So, voracious and annoyed, Lysander aspirates small findings. As in earlier days, he inhaled my scales then began sneezing as only a creature of his kind can. I feel sorry for him, but the sneezing disgusts me somewhat.

I go to the orifice where the ants emerge and signal to Lysander that there's no food. I stop in front of him, show him my crest; I convey to him that what he's eaten, what's making him sick, came from my skin, I rub up against his legs so he knows my texture, then I pick up a scale with my mouth and, gesturing wildly, I move my jaw, inhale sharply through my nose, show that what I'm about to ingest isn't food. I make as if to swallow the scale then move my tongue like I'm panting, I try to expel the scale, to vomit it up, but I don't do it right: it's already gone. Lysander looks at me with the same eyes as when we met: his pupils are shiny, sad. He doesn't understand what I've tried to act out for him. He chooses to turn and go to the living room then sits down near my companion as he tries to adjust the blinds, which are sagging from overuse.

I start to feel sick, the scale, which feels like a fingernail, is stuck in my esophagus. I think about swallowing something larger, something that would fill most of my esophagus and pull the stuck scale down as it passed through. I walk toward my companion and manage to ask him for something to eat. I want a bug with a thick body, I want a beetle, even though they're not my favorite. Like Lysander, I've grown used to the nourishment this house and its holes provide. My companion crouches to fondle the peaks of my crest; he likes to wrap his hand around my biggest horn and stroke it. I don't feel his hand when he does this, it's like if before he had touched my ponytail. My body's protrusions are insensate, as are my extremities—the only part of me that can feel is the underside of my tail. The skin is softer there, different from on my chest and stomach, which have hardened so I can creep along the floor without feeling its irregularities.

I scoured in the corners and under the furniture, found a medium-sized cockroach to save me from the intolerable prickling inside. The cockroach moved its antennae, trying to locate itself in a space which was now not the floor but the air, then it was stopped by my teeth. I lopped it in half, a yellow liquid wetting my lips, the cockroach had a familiar flavor, like my venom but lacking the sweet aftertaste. I liked it. I especially enjoyed the gentle crunch of its breaking.

When my companion saw me eat the cockroach, he said: "You're remarkable, you can now feed on things you never ate before. You're healthy." To thank him for his words, I moved my neck the way he'd asked me to the day before. If I looked straight at him and twisted my neck to one side or the other, my head took on a shape my companion found attractive.

After shedding my skin, I should have seen a doctor. I didn't, because that event and the ones that followed, which defined me as a mutating being, were healthy. It's undeniable. The delusions, however, follow their own logic; maybe that's why there are days when I don't understand how I lost my identity. Am I no longer a person?

My belly has swollen. I'm pregnant.

The present is no longer the time I'm living, I find I now lie dormant within a body that's mine but altered. While the transformation was painful—the external changes to skin, mouth, and eyes—I don't feel discomfort in my new body. To me, this life is tranquil. It's like I'm submerged in tepid water, or always under the influence of a drug that makes you happy, though within this magnificent state, there's not the slightest indication of anything artificial. I'm exactly what I most wished for, and because of that, my existence is unerring. For the same reason, time has no order: my sublimation is built on the conviction that I'm living fully.

I'm going to explain what I see in the world at this point. Outward things aren't the way I once knew them. Objects are see-through, as if made of air, their substance is strange. For example: chairs hang in emptiness. Objects have no start or end, they're linked, one can't be defined without another. Maybe I first glimpsed this when my eyelids went transparent.

To say what I said about the chairs required falsifying the image they project, because the chairs are part of the floor, the table, and space. I can't explain it any better, I give up.

Even though I said everything in the city is superimposed, an amorphous stain, my transformation has shown me there's no such error in the world's order.

My mother's death had torn from my mind any awareness of lines or individual colors: now I know black isn't singular, but can be found in red, blue, and all the hues of nature.

It was impossible to write when I was crawling, and my companion only recorded what he thought worthwhile. Just a few pages ago, he noted some details I dictated and wrote my name the way I pronounced it. That's when I fell in love with him; months before the emotion became so sonorous, I knew my companion loved me too. I didn't need much rest to repair myself and feigned sleep so he would come closer. He did it once or twice, weeks before disappearing. The last time, he sat in a chair to watch me sleep and said he didn't understand where I had come from—he was referring to my origins, my first life—then he caressed my belly and said, "I'll die without knowing you."

Of the three of us, who will die first? I wonder before I fall asleep, installed in the armchair. I deduce that as the strongest in the household, I'll see my companion die.

—

Captivity has made Lysander feeble, but he doesn't show he's unhappy because something is compelling him to remain a domestic animal. As the months have passed, I've noticed—so has my companion—that Lysander is experiencing something like old age.

XV

Fellow Creatures

The house filled with water. The bad weather fed on the air; we couldn't go outside and were confined for another winter. My companion got an electric blanket, and I stayed underneath it. I didn't eat, the weather made me despondent. Lysander now preferred the couch, since the floor's dampness gave him sores on his feet.

My belly is larger than before, but there's no way to measure its growth. I have nothing to compare it to.

It's the first day of spring. We're celebrating because the house has dried out for the most part, though some dampness remains. (I understand now that the roof has deteriorated, it doesn't fulfill its essential function: to shelter us.)

We go to the beach.

I'm spirited and healthy. The heat of the sun, newly returned to the sky, rejuvenates me. My abilities weren't affected by inclement weather or lack of appetite. This climatic shift coincides with the end of my transformation.

The spikes on the back of my neck, which give my skull a singular shape, will soon finish growing. At one time the skin that covers my shoulder blades wasn't as thick as the rest, and it burned constantly, because those spikes, stiff as bones, clawed through my back and left wounds that reopened from friction when they were just about to scar over. I tried to hang my head a little lower, looking down at the floor to minimize contact. Now, the skin on my back is thick and durable.

I'm worried about my companion. He has sudden coughing fits, and gulps of water do nothing to alleviate them. I suggested we go to the beach again, thinking the heat would heal him. He's convinced the humidity bore through his organs: "There's mold living inside me," he said. He's gone pale.

The sunlight bleaches the cliff. Its crevices hold the greatest of treasures for my kind: inside them, the rocks store their heat, so hundreds of iguanas hide there in the afternoon. I tell my companion I'm going to see them and that if he's afraid of losing me, Lysander can come. Lysander assumes his role as guard dog and follows me to the base of the cliff, where I observe my fellow creatures. As I approach, one half emerges and looks at me. I return the look, sure of myself, and she lets me inside, pulling back with enough hospitality that I get closer.

Lysander hisses and thrashes around, leaving a circle of prints in the sand. That movement, repeated again and again, frightens the creatures, who vacate the crevice slowly (they're incapable of speed). Some raise their tails toward the sky in a gesture of defiance. One inflates her dewlap so it becomes a blue balloon, its delicate surface crisscrossed with veins: she's beautiful.

I'm annoyed with Lysander; he's being rude. I go over to him and raise my tail too, I want to attack, I feel brave and spit a gob of mucusy venom at him. Lysander takes a few steps back then freezes. He doesn't know me.

I test my nails against the rock, climb a few meters up the cliff, and stay there, enjoying the light on my crest. I accept its magic and notice that my skin is the color of the stone, then realize that here, my existence could go undetected: I am part of this surface. I enter the crevice and silently rejoice—thanks to Lysander's restlessness, I have it all to myself. For a time, I am content, until I spot two eyes watching me from the depths.

XVI

Hunger

I've tried to recount what happened with clarity. There's no longer a single person who can corroborate these events. After I entered the crevice, I never saw my companion or Lysander again. I went back to the house where we lived, and the door was open. Inside, I couldn't find a single one of their belongings. The closets and drawers were empty. The blanket where Lysander slept was also gone.

Maybe Lysander called out to my companion while I was in the crevice. Perhaps my companion saw me attack that animal of my species. Perhaps he saw me devour it.

I ate one of my kind. I'm frightened, too, remembering.

—

Lately, I've been waking up with more energy. My belly continues to grow, and its thickening makes me immeasurably happy. I have the sense that my descendants will be identical to me, of unnatural similarity. It makes me feel proud. My mother and sister didn't know how to live with our unique attributes. But I did, and now I can exult in my resilience. My mutation will feed my child's heart.

Again, I heard the voice, the voice revealed I would have a daughter, and I will.

Hope is here.

The house is a kingdom all my own. I'm the master of the place. I won't betray my companion, but with his recent weakness, compounded by his ailments, I wouldn't have been guaranteed sustenance.

I couldn't trust Lysander after what he did on the beach.

What happened, and what neither I nor anyone else can attest to—the flight or disappearance of Lysander and my companion—was essential for survival. Nature protects me, just as it's meant to.

The silence in the house moves me because I was somewhere like this before, and its muteness brings my memory back to that empty, white space. The house feels like a hospital.

What's most important now is to get on my two back legs again; I achieve the equilibrium I practiced before I crawled, I walk on my feet, and my hands are once again hands that I lift to close the curtains or confirm that the protrusions crowning my spinal column are uniform. I don't want to lose the attributes I was given to stay alive. I want to take care of myself. I look for the moisturizer my companion once took from the bathroom drawer, but it's gone. In the drawer, there's only an oval mirror.

My daughter quivers inside me. She does it when I'm under the showerhead, stretching my neck so the water washes the wrinkles under my chin. Then she moves, and I think she must want to be born in the water. I picture her: she has gills, then I turn her into a bird; she, like me, is all the beasts of creation; the sum of her changes is animal history. My daughter must be an amphibian, because when I bathe, she quivers.

I can't say how many days have passed since I've been alone. I'm equal to the hours: knowing only how much time passes between one thought and another, I can calculate when the sun will rise.

I'm an adult. I look at myself in the oval mirror I found in the bathroom: I retain the attractive face I forged. The beauty of my transformation is pleasing. I notice that my body is proportional, that my hands are lovely and command respect, I think anyone would want to touch me, since skin like mine is rare, and my sense of smell is another point of pride: I can detect whoever is passing by the house. From their vapors alone, I can approximate their age, what they're digesting, and their sexual capacities.

My companion had small testicles. There are men who have small testicles because their seed is powerful.

They don't need a larger store because their line isn't in danger. My companion told me his brothers had reproduced successfully; their fleshy seeds became children when they wanted.

My companion was hard-working and knew how to keep busy: he made a radio from a piece of cardboard and some wires. I can't imagine how it works, but it was through that device that I first heard talk of the war.

My companion never found out because when they called the men to fight, he wasn't home.

I didn't mention it because my companion was incapable of killing.

He didn't kill the scorpion that bit Lysander's tail.

The anteater was delirious, near death, it seemed to me, nullified by the poison. My companion didn't avenge Lysander. He stared at the scorpion on the floor, examined its tail and the transparency of its legs. He didn't want to crush it, said: "It's too young to die." We saved Lysander by giving him big plates of lukewarm porridge to counteract his muscle spasms. He hallucinated terrifying scenes in which he died;

we saw it in the way his head trembled, in the uneven breathing that signaled a trance: his voluminous body in a state of lightness, loss.

I unraveled two cushions for the yarn. I pulled off the TV antenna and took it apart to make two needles. I'm just stopping now after days spent knitting a sweater and matching pants for my daughter. The yarn has run out, but the garment will protect her from the cold. I have to use my thick fingers to pluck out Lysander's hairs. Balling up bits of the mane he shed, I formed a spiral of hairs, it's like a small animal that reminds me of him.

I go out in search of better provisions for the birth. I've had no appetite lately, but now I need to eat. There's no one to secure sustenance for my progeny, so I have to risk myself; I have to accept the difficult labor to come.

I want to put something in writing: my happiness is so great that I can't explain it. I'm in the ideal condition for any female, not because I'm pregnant, but because

I've seen that life won't come to an end when I'm gone. If I were to lose my daughter, life would go on (somehow) because the cockroaches that have nourished me would survive. That's enough.

She's covered in a thick liquid. We still haven't formed the shell, so she's not breathing yet. When the shell begins to set, revolving inside me, she'll lose her gills and acquire new respiratory capacities. Right now, she's hungry for meat, and I'm going to buy it.

I imagine the red meat and something in my jaw contracts, my womb tightens—she's asking for what I'm thinking of.

When I had company to distract me, I didn't notice how much it unnerved me to leave the house. I miss my companion and Lysander in this moment of aloneness; I don't know if I'll make it back unharmed or if men will accost me on the way, startled if they catch a glimpse of my skin. I wear my companion's diving suit and a scarf tied securely around my neck, not an inch of skin should be visible. My eyes are covered by glasses with frames my flat nose can barely hold up. I won't make a single stop inside the grocery store; I'll go straight to the butcher.

I walk quickly, not wanting to waste time, but soon I become tired. My pregnancy claims its space; I'm no longer agile, the weight rests on my legs. I move more slowly. So far, no one has detected my strangeness, and I keep calm to avoid drawing attention.

There are lots of people at the supermarket today. It must be a day of the week they don't go to work.

I stop in front of the butcher case. There are so many portions, I don't know which to choose. I have the impulse to lengthen my neck, but I suppress the movement and quickly lower my head—I silently will myself to master my desire, which, if it can be classified at all, could only be called a roar. I am roaring; I want to command the butcher to give me meat, I have to contain myself, so I keep quiet.

My neck returns to a less conspicuous position, and I see the meat I'll ingest. A stabbing in my womb reminds me that this meat isn't just for me, that I'll share it with her. "We're getting it now, my love," I tell her softly.

—

(The egg inside me, and inside the egg, her, trembling since in my mind there's a beast that wants to attack us. But the placenta absorbs my daughter's spasms, dispelling fright from that sphere. I tame the monster; I concentrate, ask it to leave, I'm carrying the weight of millennia, and besides, I need to procure food. It goes, dragging its clumsy tail, leaving a rift in the sand. Later, that groove will turn into a river, and trees and plants will sprout up around it. In the river, fish will multiply.)

I look at the butcher, who is pounding some steaks: "I'll take this, but debone it, please." The butcher takes the package to the back of his enclosure, where he starts cutting the meat he'll give me. He doesn't look at me until he comes back with the package reassembled. He makes eye contact, tries to lean forward so he can examine my body. I pivot and flee from his gaze.

I pay for the meat at the register, keep my head down the whole time, and go home.

On the way back, I see the nurse who took care of me in the hospital. She's wearing a floral-print dress, walking hand in hand with a man. I admire the nurse. If I'd spent more time as a woman, I would have impersonated her, would have worn dresses like that. I observe her for as long as I can; when she's gone, her image remains. I understand her curative powers.

At home, I put the meat on the table. I open it then and there and begin to tear into it. The raw meat has hardly any flavor. I think a little salt might help excite me, so I go to the kitchen for some. I add salt, but not too much; pregnant women aren't supposed to have salt. I chew the pieces carefully so my daughter will get the nutrients.

The shell has begun to form. She is breathing.

While I eat the last mouthful, I feel a tooth coming loose. This happened once before, and shortly after I lost the tooth, my body created a new one. It calms me to remember that successful supplantation.

My daughter has no teeth. She has nothing even resembling bones. Her frame is cartilaginous.

She communicates using the embryo language that only a mother can understand. Her sounds are clicks of the tongue, or soft growls when she's insistent. I can't transcribe what she says, her language is primal and won't be pinned down. It makes no sense, for instance, to copy the sound of her growls— "ayhugrrrrrruiiuogrrrr." She expresses untranslatable animal emotions.

My daughter's brain is covered by a box within a larger box, just as her brain is in my womb, and both brains, mine and hers, direct my body. The first box is cartilaginous, and that's how it will remain; the second is more durable. My daughter dreams what I dream, she doesn't have memories, but she decides the endings; the substance that makes her an embryo affects them. This is how my daughter sets herself apart from me.

The shell is finished.

—

It starts to rain. When it rains, frogs are born. When we were kids, my friends and I would scoop up the tadpoles from puddles. Whoever got the biggest one in a bag won the respect of the others. When the competition was over, we returned the creatures to other puddles. We were sure, without knowing why, that those tadpoles lived alone, we never considered their mothers. But frogs never go back to their children: we were right.

My daughter now has a pair of small fins that she'll soon lose. They're the fins of our ancestors, the fish that emerged from the water. My daughter will form ribs from the bony structures of those fins; instead of swimming, she'll move like I do, in soft undulations over the earth.

She has a gland that I haven't developed. It's between her two eyes, where she'll receive the details of light. A third eye that detects luminosity, but not color.

My instincts now plot the future of a consecrated animal. I'll leave in a few days to look for a place to give birth. I prowl the corners of the house, but my daughter will be born outside. Where will I put the egg? I want it to be somewhere warm, somewhere hidden away from danger. When she's born, I'll have to leave her—once I manage to get the egg out from inside me, I'll go. There's no cruelty in this knowledge, it's simply what's done.

I had a dream. I talk about my dreams often, since they've revealed my body's mutations. I dreamed that nothing I've lived has been real. If reality dissolves in a dream, the dream is absolute. It was a dream in its purest form, in which my experiences no longer seemed to have truth to them. Again, I heard a voice dictating what I should feel. But the voice wasn't resonant, it was strange, a humming of half words or less, not even vowels. I understood anyway.

I was dreaming of my past, probably. I don't remember what I was like, but I must have looked like I did in the dream: made of white flesh, cheeks red from the cold.

Then I flew over the city where I once lived.

—

My companion was with me in the dream. He was exactly as I remembered him, but with cleaner clothes. We walked hand in hand, got off the bus, felt content when we saw the train of blue smoke it dragged through the air.

XVII

The Egg

I'm going. It's time to give birth.

I'll walk until I find the ideal place. I think if I were to leave the egg on the beach, other animals would come and eat it.

The ending starts here. This ending I remember is the seal of my animal life, the place where the vulva that ushered me in becomes visible. I'm going to be precise; I don't want to alter a single fact in this part of my testimony. I won't say anything unless it happened. I'll speak the way I know how, with the courage of an animal.

—

The truth is, Lysander left the house shortly before my companion. My companion didn't want to discuss it; the day before, he had scolded him. Lysander's fate was servitude, his loyalty ended when my companion no longer needed him to go out in public. Because a day came when my companion didn't go out anymore. He undressed and left his folded clothes on the bedroom chair.

There, from underneath his checkered blanket, he told me to close the door and never open it again.

Laying the egg was painful; I spent hours working it down the canal where I'd been keeping it, then a whole night recovering my strength, sprawled on a rock that retained a little heat. I was horrified. If I couldn't get the egg out of my body, I would lose the unlosable. This maternity made me; my only choice was to fulfill it.

I climbed a mountain, and from there, I observed the mouth of a river. I went down to see where the two waters met up close, paused, analyzed the current (dusk was reddening the water) and the abundance of fish. I thought I should wait there a few hours, until the sun reached its peak, so she wouldn't want for the heat of my insides, and that's what I did. During that time, I managed to compose myself enough to properly settle on the place where I'd lay my egg.

I chose the deformed roots of a healthy tree. There I crouched, waiting for the moment to arrive. An animal I couldn't identify paused on the opposite bank, a long-faced, moderately sized quadruped. The animal and I looked at each other.

I contracted my abdominal muscles over and over, felt that I was emptying, releasing that light weight. There was a sharp pain in my groin; the suffering lasted until the instant the egg touched the earth.

—

I got up. There she was on the ground, a sphere of ineffable whiteness. Her roundness harmonized with the curling tree roots.

XVIII

Fable

My breakfast is a piece of cheese on bread that keeps me alive. The nurse doesn't know I've been stashing the slices in my pillowcase; if I told her, they'd take my pillowcase away. I bury my nose in it to smell the bread. Nothing in this place is sad, just as my life wasn't sad before I arrived here. They admitted me for indecent exposure—or that's what they said.

I know the nurse's hands are good hands. Her voice is sweet too. She gives me what I ask for, though at times her commitment to the job gets the better of her and she betrays me to the doctor.

—

I relayed my testimony to her and said one day I'd give her this little notebook.

I don't resist when they put me to sleep with injections. At this age, I live obediently. I did what I wanted.

Sometimes, when I'm asleep, I dream of lying on the rock on that beach—I've retained my talent for dreaming of heat and feeling it. There I am, the warmth of the sun fills me with joy, I'm paralyzed by its light, but my blood continues to circulate. My companion is next to me and he's smiling: he points to Lysander, who has peed in the sand.

Today I woke up when they opened the door to my room. It was the nurse with a man I don't know.

There's nothing left here but silence.

An egg shines on my lap as if made of porcelain.

When I found out I'd be staying in the hospital, I had a nervous breakdown.

At night, once I had calmed down, I looked at

my pillow and was shocked. My eyes had left blood-colored marks on the fabric. I brought my claws to my face and felt moist scabs crusting over them. I had cried in the way of my species.

The nurse didn't accept it at first, but she had to believe me when she saw there were no injuries to justify the bleeding. My eyes were intact, and so was the skin around them.

I'll mention the relief. I'll say this metamorphosis saved my life. Never before had I felt the peace it gradually forged: I was happy.

There were only a few moments when my human nature poked through, like when I struggled to reconcile my prehistoric abilities (my remarkable skill for harnessing light or surviving without food) with the emotional fragility of men. It confused me to not feel hunger but still fret over how I'd prepare my meals. I was indecisive, and my desires didn't align; they were disjointed.

Even so, the strange internal reality that led to my body's transformation—how to elucidate the experience if not by extending it across the entire being?—still gives me chills.

Nature allowed me to be something else; virtuosic, I chose my luminous destiny.

These are days of glory. Now I dream of gardens where my body is weightless and I am a content animal. I'm proud to be chosen to dwell in these spaces, since in my dreams, I'm sure I was guided toward them deliberately, by a higher power that isn't divine, that I define as an incorporeal drive.

Nights, then, are a gift for me. And days, though lacking the beauty of those places I visit while sleeping, are also a time of peace and plenitude. I do nothing. With my love for the state of grace within the dream itself, I prefer not to move. I look at the ceiling and strive for total rigidity, no movement whatsoever of my limbs or head.

I didn't foresee the consequences of this voluntary paralysis, but they came anyway. All I wanted was undisrupted serenity, I wanted to stay happy. As the days went by and I kept insisting on stillness, my nerves began to atrophy, and I lost command of my limbs. The nurse told me that this confinement had affected my urinary tract and that I would have to position myself over a bedpan three or four times a day. I would never urinate in the usual way again.

I think I'm being deceived. The nurse is lying, she carries the bedpan away instead of emptying it in the toilet. She leaves the room with great care, not spilling a drop of the liquid, and takes my urine elsewhere.

I see her on the chair. Maybe the doctor set her there, hoping I'd get better or choose to contemplate the object instead of indulging in my dreams and my own interior. The egg looks bigger now, it has grown outside of me. I don't understand.

I tell the nurse my daughter is not a bribe and ask her to let the doctor know he can't use her to manipulate me. I demand respect, I insist: "She's my daughter and her shell can't be kept in the dark. It's white, it barely retains any heat. Tell them to take her out to the courtyard or leave her on the sidewalk in front of the hospital. And if they don't, I'll stop moving forever and die."

The nurse tells me the egg isn't on the chair, that maybe I lost track of it. At times her pronouncements strike me as incoherent, but I amuse myself by listening to the words I can't understand. "You talk like I know what you're saying," I tell her, but she goes on almost incomprehensibly. Her sentences are garbled; her reasoning, illogical; and what's more, she makes an unpleasant expression with her mouth, like she's closing her lips to signal silence. Then she tightens them, cements them together, perhaps to contain a scream.

She was also born from a woman. My emotions don't move her; she knows I'm a mother but never dares to acknowledge it in my presence. I could tell, with my atypical faculties, that she discussed the egg with my doctor. She told him that I should be discharged— since I had succeeded in laying the egg, since the egg itself was perfectly round. The doctor listened to avoid future grievances, took one of her hands in his, and kissed it like a true gentleman. With that gesture, my doctor gave the nurse's testimony its due but failed to recognize my place in the evolutionary process.

They're looking for something impossible from me. This morning, the nurse talked to me, and although I still couldn't grasp her full meaning, I did recognize two words: *real placenta*. She said something about that. But the placenta wasn't inside me. I had laid an egg, and the placenta was inside the egg, enveloping my daughter to protect her.

They drugged me, I slept for three nights or more.

Now, like before, I have trouble measuring days. I infer that two weeks have passed since I laid the egg, recorded with precision by the appearance of moles. Every seven days, a new mole appears on my chest. I count three on the skin over my heart. The moles form a scalene triangle.

I talk to the nurse, tell her I saw Lysander's destiny, tell her I should have kept him from getting lost. She's somewhat affected. She tells me to calm down, because if I don't, they'll put me to sleep again. I respond that if I'm cause for concern, it'd be best for everyone if they let me go. She shakes her head. I think if I beg, I might convince her to release me. With tremendous inner effort, I manage to fill my eyes with tears. She stares at me fixedly, asks me not to cry, but I continue. The tears slip between my scales, I whimper to give my emotions more force, give a little sob. The tears become blood, and finally, she accepts it: "You're a natural phenomenon," she says. As she leaves, she turns her head and adds, "The fact is, birth creates the womb."

That was the last time I saw her.

The next day, I sensed that my room had grown in size. Sleep and dreams had comforted me, I felt I could survive confinement as long as I needed to. I came up with a series of movements I could perform to improve my health; I crawled around the room on all fours and was cheered to see the furniture looked different from below.

Under my bed, I found the egg. The shell felt warm, and its whiteness was unchanged; it was on the floor, on top of a folded blanket. I thanked the nurse silently because she had cared for it with her soft hands, as if it were her own.

When I picked up the egg, I realized it was empty.

Daniela Tarazona (Mexico City, 1975) is the author of *The Animal on the Rock* (Deep Vellum, 2025), *Divided Island* (Deep Vellum, 2024), winner of the prestigious Sor Juana Inés de la Cruz Prize, and *El beso de la liebre*, shortlisted for the Las Américas Prize in 2013. In 2020, she published a book she cowrote with Nuria Meléndez, *Clarice Lispector: La mirada en el jardín*. Her work has been translated into English and French. She has been a fellow of Mexico's Young Artists program and is currently a member of the FONCA fund's National Network of Artists.

Lizzie Davis's recent translations include Juan Cárdenas's *The Devil of the Provinces* (longlisted for the 2023 National Book Award for Translated Literature) and *Ornamental* (finalist for the 2021 PEN Translation Prize), as well as works by Elena Medel, Daniela Tarazona, Begoña Gómez Urzaiz, and Pilar Fraile.

Kevin Gerry Dunn is a ghostwriter and Spanish/English translator of Paul B. Preciado, Cristina Morales, María Bastarós, Elaine Vilar Madruga,

Daniela Tarazona, and Paco Cerdà (*The Pawn*, Deep Vellum, 2025), among others. He has received an English PEN Award, a PEN/Heim Grant, and a National Endowment for the Arts Fellowship.